Henry and Mudge and the Great Grandpas

The Twenty-Sixth Book of Their Adventures

Story by Cynthia Rylant
Pictures by Suçie Stevenson

READY-TO-READ

ALADDIN PAPERBACKS
New York   London   Toronto   Sydney

THE HENRY AND MUDGE BOOKS

ALADDIN PAPERBACKS
An imprint of Simon & Schuster Children's Publishing Division
1230 Avenue of the Americas, New York, NY 10020
Text copyright © 2005 by Cynthia Rylant
Illustrations copyright © 2005 by Suçie Stevenson
Also available in a Simon & Schuster Books for Young Readers hardcover edition.
Designed by Lucy Ruth Cummins
The text of this book was set in 18-point Goudy.
The illustrations for this book were rendered in pen-and-ink and watercolor.
Manufactured in the United States of America
First Aladdin Paperbacks edition June 2006
10 9 8 7
The Library of Congress has cataloged the hardcover edition as follows:
Rylant, Cynthia.
Henry and Mudge and the great grandpas: the twenty-sixth book of their adventures / story by Cynthia
Rylant ; pictures by Suçie Stevenson
p. cm.—(The Henry and Mudge books)
Summary: When Henry and his dog, Mudge, go with Henry's parents to visit Great-Grandpa Bill in the
home with lots of other grandpas, they lead them all on a wonderful adventure.
ISBN-13: 978-0-689-81170-8 (hc.)
ISBN-10: 0-689-81170-5 (hc.)
[1. Old age—Fiction. 2. Dogs—Fiction.] I. Stevenson, Suçie, ill. II. Title. III. Series: Rylant, Cynthia.
Henry and Mudge books.
PZ7.R982Heamg 2005
[E]—dc21
98-18317
CIP
AC
ISBN-13: 978-0-689-83447-9 (pbk.)
ISBN-10: 0-689-83447-0 (pbk.)
1209 LAK

Contents

Grandpas

On a sunny summer day, Henry and Henry's
dog, Mudge, went with Henry's parents to
visit Great-Grandpa Bill.
Great-Grandpa Bill was very old.
He lived in a house with a lot of other
grandpas.

5

Henry liked them.
He liked their checker games and their
rocking chairs and their walking canes.

Mudge liked the grandpas too.

He liked the little mints they carried in their pockets.

When they arrived at Great-Grandpa Bill's house, Henry gave everyone a present. He always brought presents for the grandpas.

He brought books and magazines.

He brought butterscotch candies.

He brought crossword puzzles and poker cards.

The grandpas loved him.

9

They loved Mudge, too.
They petted Mudge, and when they were tired
they rested on him.

Mudge didn't mind.
He liked tired grandpas.

While Henry's father and mother went in the house to visit with all of the grandpas, Henry and Mudge set off exploring.

11

Great-Grandpa Bill's house was near the woods, and Henry couldn't wait to have fun outside.
"Let's go, Mudge!" he said.
So while everyone played checkers and cards, Henry and Mudge went looking for adventure.

13

A Pond!

Henry and Mudge walked through the
crunchy woods.
Mudge sniffed logs.
He ate sticks.
He disappeared in bushes.

15

Henry climbed on stumps.

He swung on trees.

He peeked in
little dens.

Then Henry saw a clearing.
"This way, Mudge!"
Henry and Mudge ran to the clearing.
It was beautiful!

There were meadows and flowers.

Birds and butterflies.

And a swimming pond!

"A pond, Mudge!" said Henry.
Mudge wagged and wagged.
They ran to the side of the pond.
Henry tested the water.
"Just right for swimming!"

But Henry knew they couldn't swim yet.
"No swimming alone" was one of his
parents' big rules.

"Let's go get Dad and swim, Mudge,"
Henry said.
Mudge was ready.
He was perfect at dog-paddling!

Skivvies

When Henry told his parents about the pond,
not only did Henry's dad want to swim, but
Great-Grandpa did too!
And so did the other grandpas!
They all wanted to go to the swimming pond.

"We'll have to go in our Skivvies,"
said Henry's father.
"What's 'Skivvies'?" asked Henry.
"Underwear," said his father.

Henry looked at his mother.

"No girls allowed, Mom," Henry said.

Henry's mother smiled.

"Anyway," she said, "I was going to make spaghetti for the grandpas."

"Then let's go!" said Henry.
Henry and Henry's father and Henry's big
dog, Mudge, and *all* of the grandpas went to
the swimming pond.

It took a while to get there.
The grandpas had to stop and rest on Mudge
sometimes.

When everyone got to the clearing,
Great-Grandpa Bill said, "Holy cow!"
And all of the grandpas pulled off their pants
and went swimming in their underwear.
Henry and Henry's dad did too.

Mudge gave rides to the grandpas who got tired.
"Instead of a life raft, Mudge is a *live* raft," said
Henry's father.
Henry giggled.

Everyone swam for an hour,
then they lay in the sun.

The grandpas told stories about being in the navy, or working for the railroad, or driving taxis.

One grandpa had been a singer, and he sang
them a little song.

The pond was shiny, the sun was warm, and the grass was soft.

Henry and Mudge and everyone there felt
happy.

Full and Happy

It took a while to get back to Great-Grandpa
Bill's house.

The grandpas had to rest on Mudge even more.
Mudge didn't mind.

37

When they got to the house, Henry's mother
had a big pot of spaghetti ready.
Everyone ate and ate and ate.
All of the grandpas loved spaghetti.
Especially those without teeth.

After dinner, everyone sat on the porch in
rocking chairs.
Everyone was full and happy.

The grandpas grew quiet.
Some slept.
And as the sun slowly set,
Henry and Mudge rested.
Glad for a grandpa house.